Fish Rescue

Story by Carmel Reilly
Illustrations by Alfredo Belli

Contents

Chapter 1

Hot and Dry

It was Friday afternoon.
Noah was coming home on the school bus with his friend, Harry.
Harry was sleeping over that night.

"It's so hot and dry," said Harry, looking out the window.
"We really need rain."

Noah nodded. "It's so bad on our farm that the creek has almost dried up," he said. "The native fish that live there are dying because there is not enough water."

"That's terrible!" said Harry.

"It is," said Noah.
"But I'm working hard to save those fish."

"How are you saving them?" asked Harry.

"I'm moving the fish from the creek into our dam until the rain comes," said Noah.

"Wow! That's hard work," said Harry.

"I don't mind," said Noah.
"I've been spending time at the creek since I was little. I love the native fish. It's important to look after them because they're so good for the creek's ecosystem."

At home, the boys had afternoon tea with Noah's mum.

"I'm taking Harry down to the creek," Noah said, as he finished his sandwich.

"Are you going to move some more fish?" asked Mum.

"I am!" he replied.

"And I'm going to help, too," said Harry.

Chapter 2

Catching Fish

The boys walked down to the creek.
They stood at the bank
and looked over the edge.
Instead of flowing water below,
there were only muddy puddles.

"Are there really fish in there?" Harry asked.

"Yes," Noah replied.
"And I need to move them fast
before the puddles dry up."

"How do you move them?" asked Harry.

"I'll show you," said Noah.

He waded into a puddle, crouched down and dipped his arms beneath the murky water. In seconds, he had caught a fish in his hands, and put it into a bucket.

Then he carried the bucket to the dam and let the fish go.

Harry tried to catch a fish, too.
But each one he grabbed slipped from his grasp.
"This is harder than it looks," he said.

"It takes practice," said Noah.
"But I've moved so many fish now, I'm really fast!"

"Maybe I can help by carrying the buckets to the dam instead," said Harry.

"That's a good idea," said Noah.

It was almost dark when they got back to the house.

"Harry helped me move lots of fish today," Noah said to Mum.

"That's fantastic!" said Mum.

"But there are still more in the creek," said Noah, looking miserable. "Tomorrow there's my football game, and on Sunday we're going to Grandma's. I can't move any more fish until Monday."

"Don't worry," said Mum. "Just do what you can."

On Monday afternoon, Noah went back to the creek.
As he stood on the bank, he noticed something floating just below the surface of a puddle.
It was a dead fish.

Noah felt terrible.
If he had come back sooner,
perhaps he could have saved it.
He knew he would have to work hard this week
to rescue the other fish.

Chapter 3

The Rain

The next morning, Noah woke to see dark clouds in the distance.

"I think it's going to rain today," said his mum.

Noah couldn't remember when he had last seen rain. It was hard for him to believe it would happen.

But Mum was right.
When Noah got off the school bus that afternoon,
the whole sky was dark grey.
It began to rain as he reached the house.

As the hours passed, the rain became heavier. Noah and his mum put on their coats and went down to the creek.

They could see water already starting to flow along the creek bed.

"If it keeps raining like this," said Mum, "you can move the fish back into the creek soon."

Noah grinned. "That would be amazing!" he said.

Chapter 4

The Best Reward

The following week, the local mayor visited the farm to talk to Noah.

"We've heard about your work rescuing native fish," she said. "We would like to give you a special eco-award."

Noah looked surprised.
"But how did you hear about it?" he asked.

"Your friend Harry told me," said the mayor, smiling. "He's my nephew."

The next week, Mum took Noah and Harry to the town hall to get Noah's award.

"What a great reward for all your hard work," said Mum.

"The *best* reward was being able to save the fish," said Noah.